D1645026

Dear Earth

Written by
Isabel Otter

Illustrated by
Clara Anganuzzi

For Lisa, who has always
protected the natural world ~ IO

For Mum and Dad ~ CA

CATERPILLAR BOOKS
An imprint of the Little Tiger Group
www.littletiger.co.uk
1 Coda Studios, 189 Munster Road, London SW6 6AW
First published in Great Britain 2020
Text by Isabel Otter
Text copyright © Caterpillar Books Ltd 2020
Illustrations copyright © Clara Anganuzzi 2020
A CIP Catalogue record for this book
is available from the British Library
All rights reserved · Printed in China
ISBN: 978-1-84857-941-5
CPB/1800/1340/1219
10 9 8 7 6 5 4 3 2 1

When Tessa and Grandpa went walking,
he would tell her about the Earth.

Grandpa had been an explorer once.
He had seen many wondrous things and loved
to tell Tessa about his adventures.

As Grandpa talked,
pictures were painted
in Tessa's mind.

She decided to write
a letter to the Earth.

But where
to begin?

"Start by writing 'Dear Earth',
then let your imagination flow," said Grandpa.

Dear Earth,

Tessa began.

The sea roared in the distance and Tessa continued to write...

My grandpa has told me a lot about you,

and you sound wonderful!

One day, I'm going to be an explorer, just like Grandpa.

Most of your surface is covered in water.

I want to dive into your deep oceans and see shoals of swirling fish.

I'd blow bubbles with the whales

and glide like a turtle.

I'd love to explore your lands, too.

When the animals stampede

I'd run amongst them.

My heart would
beat as loudly as their
thundering
hooves!

You are home to **gigantic** mega-beasts as well as teeny-weeny creatures.

I want to run through your meadows and kiss the butterflies...

splash
under
waterfalls

and float
in
blue
lagoons.

Part of you is
frozen over.

Do you ever
feel the **cold**?

Grandpa says that unicorns swim in the Arctic.

You have a spine of mountains that tower over everything.

Some of them have their heads in the clouds!

In the underwater forest of the mangroves, sharks keep their babies safe.

I'd like to slide down desert dunes...

but avoid the **prickly** cacti!

When the bears go fishing, I'd watch and dip my toes in the river.

Up in your rainforest canopy
I would join
in with the
screeching

hullabaloo of the birds
and monkeys.

High in the sky
I would fly with
the birds.

Soaring and swooping,

Earth, you are full of such **wonder**, but you're fragile and you need love and care.

Grandpa says that humans have hurt you...

but we can heal you too.

The sea continued to
roar in the distance
as she finished her
letter simply:

Love from
Tessa
x

Grandpa and Tessa
walked down to the
beach together.

"I wish everyone knew how
special Earth is," said Tessa.

"Do you think if people realised,
then they would want to look
after the world and keep it safe?"

"Yes, I do," said Grandpa, taking Tessa's hand.
"Perhaps if enough of us share the message,
we can still save our dear Earth."

If you want to know more...

Grandpa tells Tessa that humans have hurt our planet. He means that some people have lived – often unintentionally – in a way that has harmed the environment. We have created a lot of dirty fumes and pollution, which are bad for our world and cause it to heat up. This is known as climate change or global warming.

Earth's habitats have already started to change, affecting wildlife all over the world...

 Sea ice is melting as the Earth gets warmer. This is bad news for polar bears because they use the ice for hunting, resting and raising their cubs.

 Turtles lay their eggs on beaches. When sea ice melts, the sea level rises and begins to cover some of Earth's beaches, making life difficult for turtles.

 Plastic is thrown away in enormous amounts and, sadly, a lot of it ends up in the sea. Marine animals often choke on plastic waste mistaken for food.

 Rainforests are being cut down all over the world. Trees are very important because they clean our air and provide a home to many creatures.

But it's not all doom and gloom. We have the power to change and live in a more environmentally friendly way. There is still time to save our planet!

What can you do?

You could write or draw a letter to Earth, just like Tessa. What do you love most about the world? Are there places that you'd like to explore?

There are lots of simple ways to make a difference:

Beach clean-ups
Some beaches provide buckets and litter-pickers
at their entrances so that everyone can get involved.

Growing flowers
Bees love sweet-smelling blooms such as honeysuckle or lavender. We need
bees because they spread pollen around. This helps plants to make new seeds.

Using a walking bus for the school run
Adults walk at the front and back and everyone wears
a hi-vis jacket. This means fewer cars need to be used.

Recycling rubbish
This helps to reduce the amount of waste
that might end up in landfill or even in the sea.

Tessa asks Grandpa if people would be more likely to look after Earth once they realised how special our planet is. What do you think?

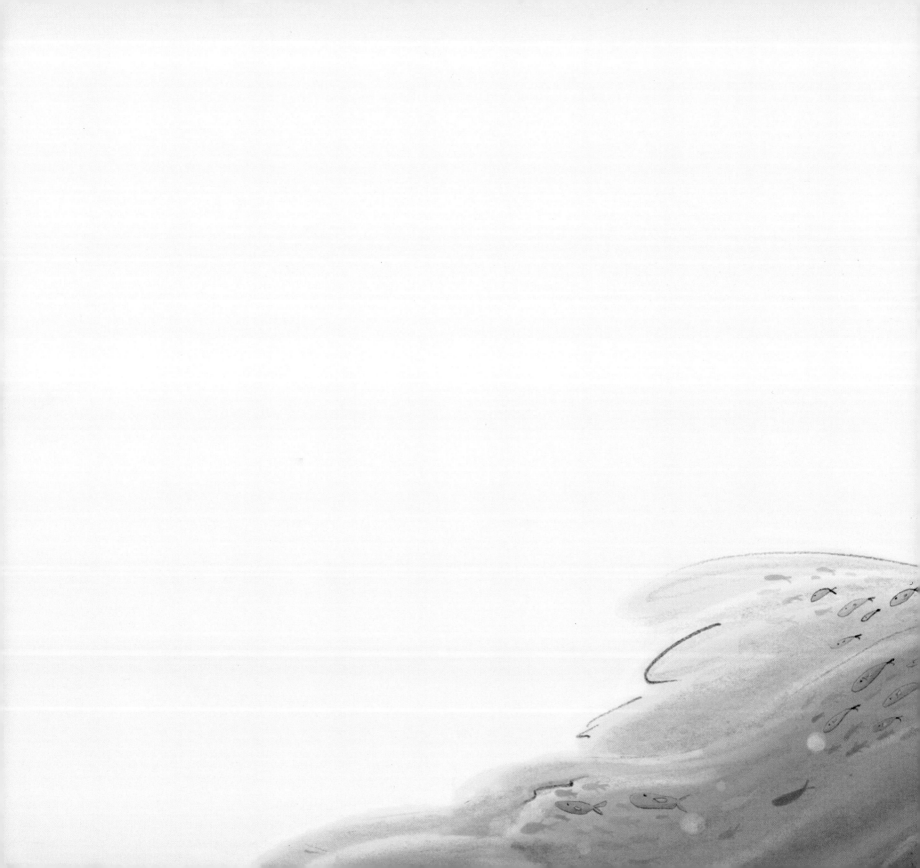